A catalogue record for this book is available from the British Library

Published by Ladybird Books Ltd
80 Strand London WC2R 0RL
A Penguin Company

2 4 6 8 10 9 7 5 3 1

© Ladybird Books Ltd MMVI

ISBN-13: 978-1-84422-955-0
ISBN-10: 1-84422-955-6

Printed in Italy

Busy Tractor

written by Jillian Harker
illustrated by Ruth Galloway

Cock-a-doodle-doo! crows the cockerel at Warner's Farm. "Wake up everyone! It's time to get to work." But in the barn, someone is already awake. An engine is chugging away beneath a bright green bonnet. Busy Tractor is waiting to make himself useful on the farm.

Who's going to need some help first? *Moo!* comes the call from the cows in the dairy. They've just been milked. Hook up the trailer, Farmer Warner! It's time to get moving.

Busy Tractor heads off to collect the milk churns. Get them loaded quickly! They have to be ready to meet the milk lorry.

Busy Tractor hurtles down the lane with his full trailer. What's that cockerel doing in the way? Move over! We can't keep the lorry waiting.

Clank, clank! go the churns as the huge wheels bump along. Look, there's the milk lorry, winding its way to the gate. Busy Tractor makes it just in time.

What needs to be done next?
Neigh! call the horses from the
paddock. They're waiting to be
fed. Busy Tractor hurries straight
back to the barn. Quick! Get the
hay onto the trailer. We can't keep
the hungry animals waiting.

Down in the paddock, the horses
prick up their ears when they hear
Busy Tractor coming. *Chug, chug!*
Breakfast is on its way!

Another job sorted out. Now it's time to give Farmer Warner a hand with the ploughing. Better hurry up and swap the trailer for the big plough, Farmer Warner!

Up and down goes Busy Tractor,
pulling the plough to make
perfect furrows. Those birds over
there look hungry. Come on down!
There are plenty of worms for
you here.

The ploughing is soon finished but Farmer Warner still needs help to sow the seeds. Off with the plough and hook on the driller. Busy Tractor will have it done in no time.

Just a minute! The birds aren't supposed to eat the seeds as well. Quick, bring the scarecrow, Farmer Warner!

There's just time for Busy Tractor's engine to cool down while Farmer Warner eats his lunch. But it isn't long before the tractor is revving up again, this time with the hedge-cutter at the ready.

Nyaaaaw! it roars, as Busy Tractor moves round the edge of the field.

Next, the grass needs to be cut. So Busy Tractor hooks up to the mowing machine in Longbottom Meadow and sets to work.
Swish! Slash! go the blades, as the square of swaying grass gets smaller and smaller.

The field mice peep out from their nest. It's time to move house. They'll find plenty of room in the hedges. The mice are soon on their way and Busy Tractor mows through the last of the grass.

Farmer Warner is tired now, but the day's work isn't over yet. Thank goodness Busy Tractor can carry him up the hill to check the sheep. This won't take long. Just sit back and enjoy the view.

Farmer Warner can look down over the whole farm from Busy Tractor's seat.

Going down the hill is easy. Busy Tractor rolls into the field by the barn to do one last job. Hook on the baler. Phew! This is heavy! It's tiring work at the end of a long day. But the hay can't be left, in case it rains. Busy Tractor soon has it all bundled up into bales.

The sun is setting as Busy Tractor trundles back into the farmyard.

The hay cart is safely stored in the barn. Perhaps Busy Tractor can settle down for the night now. Oh no! Here comes that pesky cockerel again! What could he want?

He's looking for somewhere cosy to sleep. And Busy Tractor can't say no. Can he?